MR. TICKLE

by Roger Hargreaves

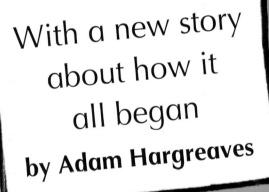

With a new story
about how it
all began

by Adam Hargreaves

EGMONT

Once upon a time ...

... there was a little boy who asked his father a question. An impossible question.

"Daddy, what does a tickle look like?"

The little boy's father scratched his head. "That's a very good question," he said.

The father sat down at his desk and opened his drawing pad.

But his mind was as blank as the page staring up at him.

So he went for a walk with the little boy and as he walked he whistled. He liked to whistle when he was thinking.

He was a very tall man.

And he had very long legs.

Extraordinarily long legs.

"Slow down, daddy," said the little boy. "Your long legs are too good at walking."

The father slowed down and then a thought came to him. If long legs were good for walking then what would be good for tickling?

Of course, long arms!

Extraordinarily long arms.

When he got home he started drawing.

And this is what he drew.

He was so pleased with his drawing he wrote a story as well.

A story that the little boy loved.

A story that you are about to read!

It was a warm, sunny morning.

In his small house at the other side of the wood
Mr Tickle was asleep.

You didn't know that there was such a thing as a
Tickle, did you?

Well, there is!

Tickles are small and round, and they have arms that
stretch and stretch and stretch.

Extraordinarily long arms!

Mr Tickle was fast asleep. He was having a dream. It must have been a very funny dream because it made him laugh out loud, and that woke him up.

He sat up in bed, stretched his extraordinarily long arms, and yawned an enormous yawn.

Mr Tickle felt hungry, so do you know what he did?

He reached out one of his extraordinarily long arms, opened the bedroom door, reached down the stairs, opened the kitchen door, reached into the kitchen cupboard, opened the biscuit tin, took out a biscuit, brought it back upstairs, in through the bedroom door and back to Mr Tickle in bed.

As you can see, it's very useful indeed having arms as long as Mr Tickle's.

Mr Tickle munched his biscuit. He looked out of the window.

"Today looks very much like a tickling day," he thought to himself.

So, later that morning, after Mr Tickle had made his bed and cooked his breakfast, he set off through the wood.

As he walked along, he kept his eyes very wide open, looking for somebody to tickle.

Looking for anybody to tickle!

Eventually, Mr Tickle came to a school.

There was nobody about, so, reaching up his extraordinarily long arms to a high window ledge, Mr Tickle pulled himself up and peeped in through the open window.

Inside he could see a classroom.

There were children sitting at their desks, and a teacher writing on the blackboard.

Mr Tickle waited a minute, and then reached in through the window.

Mr Tickle's extraordinarily long arm went right up to the teacher, paused, and then – tickled!

The teacher jumped in the air, and turned round very quickly to see who was there.

But there was nobody there!

Mr Tickle grinned a mischievous grin.

He waited another minute, and then tickled the teacher again.

This time he kept on tickling, until soon the teacher was laughing out loud and saying, "Stop it! Stop it!" over and over again.

All the children were laughing too at such a funny sight.

There was terrible pandemonium.

Eventually, Mr Tickle thought that he had had enough fun, so he gave the teacher one more tickle for luck, and then very quietly brought his arm back through the open window.

Chuckling to himself, he jumped down from the window, leaving the poor teacher to explain what it was all about.

Which of course he couldn't.

Then Mr Tickle went to town.

And what a day Mr Tickle had.

He tickled the policeman on traffic duty at the crossroads in the middle of town.

It caused an enormous traffic jam.

He tickled the greengrocer just as he was piling apples neatly in his shop window.

The greengrocer fell over backwards, and the apples rolled all over the shop.

At the railway station, the guard was about to wave his flag for the train to leave.

As he lifted his arm in the air, Mr Tickle tickled him.

And every time he tried to wave his flag, Mr Tickle tickled him, until the train was ten minutes late leaving the station and all the passengers were furious.

That day Mr Tickle tickled everybody.

He tickled the doctor.

He tickled the butcher.

He even tickled old Mr Stamp the postman, who dropped all his letters into a puddle.

Then Mr Tickle went home.

Sitting in his armchair in his small house at the other side of the wood, he laughed and laughed every time he thought about all the people he had tickled.

So, if you are in any way ticklish, beware of Mr Tickle and those extraordinarily long arms of his.

Just think. Perhaps he's somewhere about at this very moment while you're reading this book.

Perhaps that extraordinarily long arm of his is already creeping up to the door of this room.

Perhaps it's opening the door now, and coming into the room.

Perhaps, before you know what is happening, you will be well and truly …

… tickled!